For Aidan
—S. F.

For Jen
—C. S.

atheneum

ATHENEUM BOOKS FOR YOUNG READERS
An imprint of Simon & Schuster Children's Publishing Division
1230 Avenue of the Americas, New York, New York 10020
ATHENEUM BOOKS FOR YOUNG READERS is a registered
trademark of Simon & Schuster, Inc.
Atheneum logo is a trademark of Simon & Schuster, Inc.
For information about special discounts for bulk purchases, please
contact Simon & Schuster Special Sales at 1-866-506-1949 or
business@simonandschuster.com.
The Simon & Schuster Speakers Bureau can bring authors to your live
event. For more information or to book an event, contact the Simon &
Schuster Speakers Bureau at 1-866-248-3049 or visit our website at
www.simonspeakers.com.
Book design by Ann Bobco
The text for this book is set in Requiem.
The illustrations for this book are rendered in pencil and colored
digitally.
Manufactured in China
0115 SCP
First Edition
10 9 8 7 6 5 4 3 2 1
Library of Congress Cataloging-in-Publication Data
Ferrell, Sean.
I don't like Koala / Sean Ferrell ; illustrated by Charles Santoso. — 1st ed.
p.   cm.
ISBN 978-1-4814-0068-8 (hardcover)
ISBN 978-1-4814-0069-5 (eBook)
[1. Toys—Fiction. 2. Koala—Fiction.] I. Santoso, Charles, illustrator.
II. Title. III. Title: I don't like Koala.
PZ3673Iad 2015
[E]—dc23   2013015976

I DON'T LIKE KOALA

words by Sean Ferrell · pictures by Charles Santoso

ATHENEUM
Books for Young Readers
New York London Toronto Sydney New Delhi

Adam does not like Koala.

Koala is the most terrible terrible.

He has terrible eyes that follow Adam
everywhere he goes.

Adam tries to explain to his parents . . .

"I don't like Koala."

But they don't understand.

Every night when it is time
to go to bed, Adam has
the same routine:

He takes a bath.

He puts on his pajamas.

He brushes his teeth . . .

and he tries to get rid of Koala.

Adam puts Koala away.
Away is a lot of different places.

But every morning
when Adam wakes up . . .

Koala is always there.
In his bed.
On his pillow.

Closer than close.

"I don't like Koala."

Father says, "Don't play with Koala like that or you'll lose him."

"I don't like Koala!"

Mother says, "Don't leave Koala behind.
You know how you'd miss him."

"I don't like Koala!"

After snack time, Father says,
"You must have loved your snack.
You ate every bite."

"What snack?" asks Adam.
"Oh, maybe it was Koala,"
   says Father.

Adam is sick
and tired
of Koala.

He takes Koala on a long, long walk.

They climb hills.

They walk around rocks.

They wander among trees.

And when Adam is certain
Koala isn't looking . . .

he runs away.

Among trees.

Around rocks.

Over hills.

All the way home.

And there is Koala.

That night, as Adam dresses for bed, he knows
there is nothing worse than Koala.

Koala is the most terrible terrible.
He has a terrible face.
And terrible paws.
And terrible eyes that follow him everywhere.
Watching and watching.

Watching and watching for . . .

a MORE terrible terrible?

Gulp.

Maybe Koala isn't so terrible after all.

Adam makes sure Koala is comfortable.
He makes sure he is closer than close.
And right before he goes to sleep,
he whispers,

"I love Koala."